Jingle's
Big Race

A Bugleberry Book™

Written by Ruth Brook
Illustrated by Vala Kondo

Troll Associates

Library of Congress Cataloging in Publication Data

Brook, Ruth.
   Jingle's big race.

    Summary: With the help of her supportive friends,
Jingle competes in the Fun Run Race, hoping to win the
gold medal.
    [1. Running—Fiction.   2. Racing—Fiction.   3. Friend-
ship—Fiction] I. Kondo, Vala, ill. II. Title.
PZ7.B78964Ji   1988   [E]   86-30729
ISBN 0-8167-0902-5 (lib. bdg.)
ISBN 0-8167-0903-3 (pbk.)

One summer morning, when the Bugleberries were playing catch in Piccolo Park, they saw a big sign tacked up on the old elm tree.

Skip stood on his tiptoes, so he could read the words:

COME ONE, COME ALL!!!
Join in the Fun Run Race
around Woodwind Lake.
Saturday morning at 10 o'clock
GOLD MEDAL FOR WINNER

"Fun is fun! But what's a Fun Run Race?" asked Toony.

Betty explained. "People run around the lake as fast as they can. The one who runs fastest of all wins the race. Since it's fun to run, it's called a Fun Run Race."

"I know what would be fun," said Bo. "It would *really* be fun if one of us could run in the race."

"Hmmm," thought Jingle, "it sure would be."

For the rest of the day, Jingle thought about running in the race.

She thought about it while she was watching TV.

She thought about it while she was eating her dinner.

And when she went to sleep, she dreamed that she ran faster than anyone else and that she won the gold medal!

The next day, Jingle told everyone that she had made an important decision.

"I'm going to run in the race," she said. "I'm going to run faster than anybody else. And *I'm* going to win the gold medal!"

Then Jingle showed her friends a book she borrowed from the library. It was called GET READY TO RUN. Jingle read:

Practice running every day.
Exercise and stretch your muscles.
Eat healthful food.
Get lots of rest.
Wear good running shoes.

Jingle got up very early the next morning. She put on her blue sweat suit and her sneakers.

"I sure wish I had a pair of Flying Skidoo shoes," she thought as she tied her old sneakers.

After a good breakfast, Jingle went outside. She stretched her arms and legs. She did eight jumping jacks, and she touched her toes ten times.

Just then, the Bugleberries passed by.

"Look at Jingle!" squealed Toony. "Jingle's upping and downing!"

"I guess she's really serious about the race," said Rosie.

But Jingle did not notice her friends. She started to run down Horn Lane.

The Bugleberries went off to play hide-and-seek.

Jingle ran all the way down Horn Lane, around to Flute Street, and back along Buglebend Boulevard. She ran past McBugle's Bugleburger, past the Trumpet Toy Emporium, past the Bugle Shoe Boutique, all the way to the library and back.

By the time Jingle turned up Horn Lane, she was very tired and out of breath.

Jingle stopped to rest in front of Dolly's house. The other Bugleberries were having a picnic in the garden.

"Hey, Jingle," Dolly called. "I made some coconut crisp cookies. Do you want one?"

Jingle really wanted a coconut crisp cookie, but she knew that she shouldn't eat too many sweets. Not if she wanted to win the Fun Run Race!

"No thanks," Jingle sighed.

Every day that week, Jingle worked a little harder. The Bugleberries had stopped asking her to play with them.

While they looked for worms, Jingle touched her toes.

While they played dress up, Jingle did sit ups.

While they built a go-cart, Jingle ran and ran and ran.

On the day before the race, the telephone rang. It was Betty.

"Hey, Jingle," she said. "We're having a swimming party. Forget that silly race and come on over."

"I can't go," Jingle said. "Today's my last day to practice. Tomorrow is the race and I want to win!" She hung up the phone.

Jingle felt upset. She loved to swim and she missed her friends, but she didn't want to quit now!

Jingle put on her running clothes. But, just as she was tying her shoelaces, she saw a big hole in the sole of her sneaker.

"Oh, no!" she cried. "Now I'll never win!"

Jingle went outside and sat in her yard. All the other Bugleberries were playing in Betty's pool. Jingle could hear them laughing and splashing and having a wonderful time.

Her eyes filled with tears. She hid her face in her hands and sobbed.

Toony peeked through the bushes.

"Look!" she said. "Jingle is crying!"

The Bugleberries jumped out of the pool
and ran over to see what was wrong.

When Jingle saw her friends, she cried
even harder.

"I feel so sad," she sobbed. "You're all
having such a good time and I can't play
with you. I feel lonely and tired, and now I
have a hole in my sneaker, and I won't be
able to run fast enough. And the worst part
is, nobody seems to care whether I'm in the
race or not."

Jingle went back to her house and slammed the door. The Bugleberries felt terrible.

"Jingle thinks we don't care about her," said Betty.

"Poor Jingle," sighed Rosie. "We should not be playing. We should be helping her."

"Poor, poor Jingle," said Toony. "I'll give her my little sneakers."

"Wait a minute!" cried Skip. "I have an idea!"

All the Bugleberries got into a huddle and made a special plan.

17

Betty ran to her house and took the big hippo bank down from her shelf.

Dolly opened her treasure chest and took out all her birthday money.

Bo borrowed money from his big brother and promised to bring him breakfast in bed for six months.

Toony took the quarters the tooth fairy had left under her pillow.

Rosie picked some flowers and sold them to her neighbor.

Skip went to the Bugle Bank
and took out his life savings.
   Together, they all went to
the Bugle Shoe Boutique.
   When they came out, they
were carrying a box all
wrapped in shiny paper.

The Bugleberries went straight to Jingle's house and rang the bell. Jingle opened the door.

"Surprise! Bugleberries to the rescue!" they shouted.

Bo gave Jingle the box wrapped in shiny paper.

When Jingle opened the box, she could
hardly believe her eyes. Inside was the most
beautiful pair of red, white, and blue Flying
Skidoo running shoes, and a card that said:

To our dear friend, Jingle.
Good luck tomorrow.
We're proud of you,
and we love you.

Jingle looked at her friends and smiled.
Then she put on her new running shoes.
They fit perfectly!

On the morning of the race, all the
runners gathered at Woodwind Lake.

"I didn't know there would be so many
people," said Dolly.

"I didn't know there would be so many
grownups," said Jingle.

"They sure have long legs," Betty said.

"They sure look fast," said Rosie.

Jingle's heart was pounding. "I can do it,"
she repeated to herself. "I can win this
race!"

All the runners stood behind the starting line. The judge stepped up on the platform and blew the bugle.

"Get ready! Get set! Go!" he called.

Everyone was off and running.

A woman with red shorts ran way ahead.

A man in a yellow shirt almost knocked Jingle down. But Jingle kept on running.

The Bugleberries cheered. "Go, Jingle, go! You can do it! Keep it up!"

The runners ran into the woods and disappeared.

The Bugleberries walked to the finish line and waited. After a while, the crowd began to cheer. The first runner was coming around Woodwind Lake.

"Is it Jingle?" cried Betty.

Skip stood on his tiptoes and looked at the runner.

"I can't see," he said.

"It's somebody tall," said Toony.

"Somebody too tall to be Jingle!" sighed Rosie.

The winner ran across the finish line. Everyone cheered and clapped and patted her on the back.

"It's not Jingle," said Rosie. "Jingle didn't win!"

One by one, the runners crossed the finish line. The Bugleberries waited, but there was no sign of Jingle.

And then, there was Jingle, running as fast as she could, right across the finish line!
The Bugleberries cheered. Then they shouted, "Hooray for Jingle!"

Jingle walked toward them. She sat on the grass and tried to catch her breath.

"I didn't win," she said sadly.

Everybody told Jingle that she had done a good job. Everybody was proud that Jingle had finished the race, even though she hadn't won it.

"But now I won't win the medal," Jingle said.

After the last runner had come in, the judge blew his bugle.

"It's time to give out the medals," he called.

"Medals?" Jingle said. "I thought there was only one medal."

First, the judge gave a medal to the winner of the race. Then, he gave a medal to the fastest runner over sixty years old.

At last, the judge had one medal left. "Ladies and gentlemen," he said, "the fastest runner under the age of ten is JINGLE!"

"Jingle!" cried the Bugleberries. "Jingle, you won. You won a medal!"

Jingle went up to the platform. The judge put the medal around her neck and shook her hand.

"Thank you," said Jingle. "I worked very hard, but I could not have done it without the help of my friends, the Bugleberries."

Everybody clapped and shouted, "Hooray for the Bugleberries! Hooray for Jingle!"